Little Charity

By Rose Sprinkle

Illustrations by Maryury Rivera

RESOURCE *Publications* · Eugene, Oregon

Little Charity was
The most selfish of elves,
Who loved making presents
But just for herself.

"Give away all these toys?
It just isn't fair!
I could never part with them
Or possibly share!"

"I tinker and toil and
Make gifts all day long.
They should stay here with me,
Where they truly belong."

"I'll show them this Christmas;
I'll show them alright!
These toys will be mine
By the end of this night."

So when no one was looking,
The naughty little elf
Snuck into Santa's workshop
And stole toys off the shelf.

"I'll take the blocks and teddy bears
And, don't mind if I do,
These puzzles and red bicycle
are all coming too."

She stuffed her bag full
With every last toy
That all had been made
For good girls and good boys.

All the elves gathered
To make ready Christmas Day,
To sort all the presents
And load Santa's sleigh.

But with no toys in sight,
The gift-drop tradition
Would soon prove to be
An impossible mission!

"Christmas is ruined!
What will we do?
Without any gift wrap
And presents so few?"

But Santa just laughed
In his old jolly way
And assured the sad elves
They could save Christmas Day.

"You don't think I know
Who's been naughty or nice?
There's just one little thief
That's behind this toy heist."

With his magic snow globe
And a shake and a twirl,
Little Charity was summoned
And appeared in a whirl.

"My dear Little Charity,
What's the meaning of this?
Your name's clearly inked
Tip-top of the naughty list."

"Santa, I know what I did,
And it was pretty bad,
But giving up presents
Makes me feel really sad."

"I love all the ribbon
And sparkles and fun,
And I can't give them up,
No, not even one!"

"It's time that you learn
The true meaning of Christmas
Has little to do
With your holiday wish list."

"Now, on Dasher, on Dancer,
On Prancer and Vixen!
Our little elf friend
Needs some holiday fixin'."

The sleigh flew up
And into the sky,
Over villages and houses
That quickly passed by.

Far from the North Pole,
They finally arrived
At a little brick house
With a family inside.

There were four little stockings
All hung in a row,
And the family was gathered
'round the fire's warm glow.

But Little Charity noticed
Not four kids, but three,
All hanging their heads
and on bended knee.

"Please bless me, Jon and Judy,
And Mommy and Daddy,
But most of all our dear May,
Who's not here with our family."

"She's far from her home,
Across the big sea,
Spending Christmas abroad
While serving her country."

"I'd gladly give up
All my presents and gifts
just to let sister know
how dearly she's missed."

Little Charity felt tears
Fall down from her cheek
As she saw this sweet child
So humble and meek.

"I've been so self-centered,
Only thinking of me,
When these presents were meant
To help others in need."

"Santa, I think we can help
With this one Christmas wish.
I remember a postcard
Addressed to 'big sis'!"

"That's the spirit, little one!
You're beginning to learn
To give without expecting
Anything in return."

So, in a rush, they traveled
Across the ocean blue
To deliver a letter
To a soldier . . . or two.

Little Charity smiled
With the biggest of grins
As she felt her heart warm
From a joy deep within.

"Well done, Little Charity,
But that's just the beginning.
We have the whole night
To spread the spirit of giving."

So off they went
All over the globe,
From Iceland to Ireland,
To Japan, then to Rome.

The reindeer flew
'til the rise of the sun,
Delivering their gifts
'til the very last one.

And so, Little Charity learned
A love that's profound—
That by thinking of others,
There is joy to be found.

www.thelittlevirtues.com

Resource Publications, An Imprint of Wipf and Stock Publishers 199 W. 8th Ave., Suite 3 Eugene, OR 97401
www.wipfandstock.com

Cataloguing-in-Publication data:

Names: Sprinkle, Rose, author | Rivera, Maryury Illustrator
Title: Little Charity / Rose Sprinkle.
Description: Eugene, OR: Resource Publications, 2021
Identifiers: ISBN 978-1-6667-3587-1 (hardcover) | ISBN 978-1-6667-9349-9 (paperback) | ISBN 978-1-6667-9350-5 (ebook)
Subjects: LCSH: Children's Stories | Adventure and adventurers—Fiction | Coming of age—Fiction

CPSIA information can be obtained
at www.ICGtesting.com
Printed in the USA
LVHW012349241121
704178LV00002B/3

9 781666 735871